THE
DEVIL
YOU KNOW

THE LIZZIE HOLLAND STORIES

BOOK ONE

Samantha Turner

ISBN 9798640151817
Published by Amazon UK

CONTENTS

Chapter One 1

Chapter Two. 5

Chapter Three. 7

Chapter Four 9

Chapter Five. 11

Chapter Six. 13

Chapter Seven 16

Chapter Eight 18

Chapter Nine 20

Chapter Ten 24

Chapter Eleven. 27

Chapter Twelve. 30

Chapter Thirteen 34

Chapter Fourteen 37

Chapter Fifteen 40

Chapter Sixteen 42

Chapter Seventeen 43

Chapter Eighteen. 46

Chapter Nineteen. 47

Chapter Twenty 49

Chapter Twenty-one 50

CHAPTER ONE

The blinding glare of the fluorescent tubing lights was giving Lizzie a headache again. The constant flickering plus the annoying tinny, tapping sound made her want to smash the damned thing. Not a good idea as the glass can splinter and blind you. After twenty-three years of working here, you would expect her to be used to those horrible lights. You would also think someone would be sent from head office to change the bulb, but no. Not until they were working by candlelight would anything be fixed in this box of doom. The box of doom, that is what Lizzie liked to call the pharmacy where she had spent the best years of her life. A flat-roofed, glass-fronted tiny little building on the corner of a council estate, roasting hot in the summer and cold in the winter. Having left community high school with average GCSE results and no clue as to what to do next, Lizzie's mum scoured the local job pages until she found a suitable position for her youngest daughter. The job was exciting when Elizabeth first started at the pharmacy, dispensing medicines that she had never even heard of, serving customers, and learning about how different drugs acted on the body. Not working was never an option in the Evans' household. As a working-class family living in the

North West, they did not have much money. Both Lizzie and her elder sister Amber had been expected to find a job as soon as they left school. Although her parents worked full time in the local Heinz factory life was a struggle financially. College and university were never an option. Get a job and earn your keep, simple as that. There was no money for airy-fairy dreams or ambition. So, Groundhog Day it was for Lizzie. Five days a week, the same people, the same place, the exact same routine. For twenty-three long years. Outside of the box of doom, life inevitably happened. Girly holidays abroad and nights out at the clubs in town, doing what most young people Lizzie's age were doing. One warm night in May while out with friends, Lizzie met a local lad called David Holland. He was four years older with blonde hair and deep brown eyes; they hit it off immediately and soon became inseparable. Lizzie's parents got on well with David and vice versa. After a long engagement, Lizzie and David were married in a small ceremony and moved into a modest house on the outskirts of town. David also worked in a factory, and it was hard graft for the minimum wage, but he never complained and compared to his days in the army this job was easy. Although they never had any children or lots of money, Lizzie and David were happy and very much in love. Lizzie had her hiking and David had his politics. He was very opinionated and liked to argue about controversial subjects online. These heated discussions kept him occupied. The only thing spoiling Lizzie's contentment was her job in the pharmacy. It was a stressful occupation with not enough staff to cover the workload, and the insidious dread had been creeping up inside her for years, causing anxiety and panic attacks. 'There has to be more to life than this', Lizzie would whine repeatedly. She wanted to be inspired to use her creativity, but no one wanted to know. She was dreaming, her family said, and everyone hates their job. You just get on with it. Better the devil you know blah blah blah and Lizzie was sick of hearing it. The Evans family do not take risks, do not like change. 'Ambition isn't for people like us', they said.

After many months of pondering and battling self-doubt, Lizzie decided she was going to leap. She would leave her safe, familiar job, ignore the prophets of doom in her ear, and risk making a fool of herself in the hope of breaking free. Now all she had to do was pluck up the courage to tell everyone and brace herself for the onslaught of negativity.

If Lizzie had been the kind of person to give in to pressure and doubt, then maybe she would have listened to her parents and her sister when they told her she was being ridiculous and having a mid-life crisis. Lizzie however, was stubborn, and had made up her mind. It wasn't a decision she had made lightly, and she and David had discussed it at length. He wasn't over the moon about it, but he was willing to support her as he had seen how the job had been affecting Lizzie's mental health lately. With nervous excitement and a little sadness, Lizzie gave in her notice at the pharmacy. Saying a teary goodbye to colleagues and customers who had also become friends over the years, she walked out of the doom box for the final time. Lizzie would kind of miss the old place; it had been a big part of her life since she was a teenager, and many of the customers had watched her grow up. Now was the time to move on, though. The time for a new adventure had arrived.

CHAPTER TWO

Lizzie was not going to spend the next twenty-five years in another humdrum job that she would hate. After searching the internet, she came across a fully funded NVQ 3 college course to become a nail technician, to learn how to apply all kinds of artificial nails and designs. This course was perfect! It was creative and could lead to Lizzie having her own mobile business one day.

By advertising on social media, posting leaflets through doors, and promoting special offers, she could become a success. This course could be just the thing she had been hoping to find.

After sixteen weeks, the nail technician course was complete, and Lizzie was eager to go with her new business venture. Instagram, Facebook, and local advertising had given her a regular client base, and Lizzie enjoyed the interaction with new people. Armed with her satellite navigation and her box of tricks, she would drive to the house of the client to create all kinds of fabulous false nails.

Lizzie was always a little apprehensive before going to a new client's house for the first time, but they were very welcoming and offered her a coffee. On that particular morning, though, after receiving a message on her Facebook business page to go to the house of seventeen-year-old Leanne Parker, Lizzie's nerves were a little more profound than usual. She could not say why. Leanne seemed friendly enough, and her online profile was the kind you would expect. There was just something unnerving Lizzie, maybe because the address was a bit secluded. No, she was being silly, and the old anxiety was just popping up today. Her business was important, and she could not afford to turn down a perfectly good client on a wobble of nerves.

CHAPTER THREE

Roy Peters cursed as his internet connection crashed again. The signal in this countryside area was crap, and the Wi-Fi was virtually non-existent. After turning everything off at the wall and waiting for thirty seconds, thankfully it seemed to be up and running again. Eagerly he logged back on to his Facebook account and began scrolling through the newsfeed. Roy had lived alone since his elderly parents passed away. With no siblings, the run-down cottage and surrounding two-acre garden belonged to him. Not short of money, Roy had been left a substantial inheritance but had no interest in spending it on the house.

Facebook was almost like having friends and kept Roy company in his secluded existence. He could be anyone he wanted online, and no one would ever know who the real person behind the keyboard was. Of course, Roy did not have any friends, online or otherwise. He had always been a bit different, odd some might say. As a child, the nasty little boy liked to keep insects in jars and watch them struggle frantically to escape until finally, the air ran out, and they lost the fight and died. It excited him that he had power over their fate.

As a keen hunter, Roy often went out at night with his shotgun. The area was abundant with wild deer and rabbits, foxes, and pheasants. Although he enjoyed the thrill of stalking the animals, for Roy, it was all over too quickly: bang, one shot, and the animal was dead. He had needed more and more kills to keep up the excitement. Maturing into adulthood saw him discover the dark side of the internet, where Roy Peters moved on to a more sinister form of entertainment. He fed his evil desires by watching violent snuff videos where victims are tortured and murdered on camera. Roy was a virgin, too shy to approach a woman, too weird for any woman to approach him: so, these vile recordings aroused the dominating sexual part of his sick personality.

Living alone in the Lancashire countryside, no one could know what Roy was planning in that sick mind of his. The internet was not enough. He wanted a real person in this house. The very thought of them vulnerable and alone, wide-eyed, and frightened in his control made him dizzy with anticipation.

CHAPTER FOUR

Lizzie's reliable little Fiat bumped along the rough country lane as she tried to avoid the many potholes. This house certainly was out of the way. Green fields and hills stretched out on either side, the sky dark with threatening clouds on the horizon. A posh robotic voice told her she was just three minutes away from reaching her destination. Thank the Lord she thought; it had not been an easy place to find despite the sat nav, and Lizzie was more than ready for a coffee and the bathroom. Rowan Cottage finally came into view, and Lizzie could see the old place had not been modernised.

The lone cottage built of grey stone had a traditional wooden front door and a brass letterbox. The door had once been a pretty, red colour, but now only faded bits of peeling paint remained. The four windows also had wooden frames that were damp and crumbling, the glass all dirty and old.

This wreck of a house was not the kind of place she would expect a young, image-conscious girl to live. But who was Lizzie to judge? Maybe Leanne's parents did not have much money, or the house was nicer inside. It wasn't any of her business.

Taking her box of supplies out of the car boot, Lizzie made her way to the front door of the cottage and knocked firmly. Looking around her, she could see a large garden full of nettles and prickles. If they were not going to mow it, maybe they could scatter wildflower seeds, she thought.

The sudden creak of the door brought Lizzie back to the moment. In front of her stood a balding, chubby man about fifty-odd years old wearing brown cord trousers and a bobbly green jumper. His skin looked pale and sallow with eyes small and beady like a snake.

'Hello', said Lizzie. 'I've got an appointment with Leanne Parker; I hope I have the right address'.

CHAPTER FIVE

Amber Evans opened her bleary eyes and tried to focus them on the bedside clock. Seven am. 'Urghh', she sighed. Amber was not a morning person. At forty-five, she was four years older than her sister Lizzie. Her auburn hair had started to show signs of grey, and her pale, freckled complexion screamed for more Botox even though no one else seemed to agree. Ageing was not going to stop Amber looking her best, if only she could afford the expensive treatments. Working as a shop assistant would never make her a millionaire, to be quite honest she didn't want to work at all. Amber wanted to be a lady of leisure with a wealthy husband and his limitless credit card in her purse.

As children, Amber and Lizzie would have vicious cat fights, tearing out fists of hair before their Mum or Dad pulled them apart. As they grew up though, Lizzie and Amber became best friends, so Amber felt a little lost when David turned up. He was a nice lad who adored Lizzie, but Amber could not help feeling a bit resentful. Amber had not been lucky in love; she was quite fussy, and no one seemed to meet her high expectations. After a few failed relationships, she had given up looking for Mr Right. When Lizzie and David got married, it was like a kick in the teeth. Amber was the eldest; it should have been her.

The years passed, and Amber would often meet Lizzie for coffee and lunch. They would visit each other's houses and spend time together with their parents. It was never long before the conversation turned to both sisters complaining about work. Amber may not have the same stress that Lizzie had, but working at the DIY store was boring. The only benefit was the discount on paint and wallpaper. Lately though, Lizzie had begun to get on Amber's nerves; maybe it was the antidepressants she was taking, but Lizzie had suddenly become all positive and hopeful. Amber used to like the fact that they both hated their jobs: it gave her comfort that Lizzie was just as unhappy and negative. There was camaraderie in their despair. Now Lizzie was spouting all kinds of rubbish, 'anything is possible'. 'Be thankful for what you have'. 'It's never too late to change your life'. Yea right. She was on another planet!

Lizzie did change her life though, and surprise surprise; everything landed on her lap as usual. Now a qualified nail technician, she chose her hours and was making a steady income faffing around doing arty nails and drinking coffee all day. It was alright for some! Knowing Lizzie, she would end up with a salon, become rich, and get all the things that Amber wanted. It wasn't fair at all.

CHAPTER SIX

Hearing a knock on the front door, Roy peered through the yellowing net curtain and saw a red Fiat Punto parked up outside; this must be her. His palms started to sweat, and he had to compose himself before answering the door. 'Stay calm', he told himself. 'Everything is in place: this is what you wanted'. Roy opened the door and saw the woman that he had been secretly stalking via Facebook for the last four weeks. Lizzie Holland was pretty and didn't look her age; her ample breasts stood out against her small, slightly chubby stature and large hazel eyes made her appear innocent like a doe. She wore a plain white t-shirt and fitted blue jeans that clung perfectly to her wide hips.

Pushing a strand of long brown hair from her face Lizzie smiled and introduced herself.

'Oh, yes, of course, please come inside', said Roy.

The first thing that Lizzie noticed when entering the run-down cottage was the smell – old fashioned and musty due to the damp and black mould that was visible around the windows and in the corner of the walls. The carpet that ran through the living room and up the stairs was brown with yellow patterns, threadbare in places, and looked like it needed a thorough vacuuming. There was a shabby beige sofa positioned in front of a real fire and an old-fashioned rocking chair in the corner. A mahogany side table stood next to it with a tassel shaded lamp. There were no family photographs at all. Not even one, which seemed odd to her for a man who had a teenage daughter. Everything about the room was old except the television and Skybox.

'My daughter Leanne is on her way home from college; she has a half-day today but is running a bit late. I'm sure she won't be too long; can I make you a drink while you wait?' Roy asked in a softly spoken voice.

'A black coffee, no sugar would be lovely thanks'. 'Would it be alright if I used your bathroom first, though? It was quite a drive to find you'.

'Up the stairs, along the landing and it's the door at the bottom', Roy replied.

This was going to be even better than he anticipated. He could quickly drop the Rohypnol drug into the coffee without the risk of being detected.

On entering the bathroom, a nauseating green suite greeted Lizzie, limescale, and dust in abundance.

'Let's get this over with', she thought.

Making her way back down the stairs, Lizzie hoped there would be a table of some sort where she would be able to work. She would need space to set up all the nail equipment for Leanne. The aroma of strong coffee hit her nostrils as Lizzie re-entered the living room where a surprisingly clean cup was handed to her.

'Thank you; sorry, I don't know your name'.

'Roy, I'm Roy, Leanne's Dad. She won't be much longer'.

The ticking antique clock on the mantelpiece only added to the uncomfortable silence. Two thirty-one pm; she would wait until three, and if Leanne was not here by then, she would make her excuses and leave. This cottage was giving her the creeps, and there was something a bit off about Roy; he kept staring at her and asking if her coffee was strong enough. He was making Lizzie feel awkward and self-conscious.

CHAPTER SEVEN

T en pm. Finally, David's shift was over. It had been a busy eight hours at the factory, and he had needed to fix a few problems with the machines, causing even his well-built arms to ache a little. Not to worry, soon he would be home. Lizzie will have a freshly brewed coffee and a cuddle waiting. Lizzie would usually text David about six o'clock when she knew he would be on his tea break, but he had not heard from her tonight. She must have had a late client or something.

As he turned the key in the white PVC door to their home, David walked into a silent and dark living room. No coffee. No Lizzie. This behaviour was strange and out of character for her. He turned on the lights and walked around the house, searching each room and calling Lizzie's name. Taking his mobile phone from his pocket, he dialled Lizzie's number only to be answered by her voicemail. A slight panic was growing in his stomach now, but David tried to keep calm and rational. Sitting down on the cream suede sofa, he phoned Lizzie's Mum, then her sister, and then her two best friends, but they hadn't heard from her either. He felt bad for worrying them, but he had to find out where Lizzie could be. The police would not do anything yet as it was too soon to file a missing person report. A thought occurred to David, Facebook. He would check when Lizzie had last been active on her page and check her business account for any client appointments. Maybe she had rushed off and not had time to charge her phone or the car had broken down somewhere. Nine hours ago, Lizzie had not been active on Facebook for nine hours. That was worrying, but if her mobile had died then, of course, she could not access her account. Still, nine hours was a long time for Lizzie to be out even if David was right about the car.

On Lizzie's business account, David could see a list of clients she had booked in today. The last one had been to a Leanne Parker of Rowen Cottage, Brierley Lane, at two pm. Brierley Lane; David had not heard of it and used Google maps to look it up. It was about a twelve-mile drive out into the country, off the beaten track with rough scrubland and not much else nearby. There was a telephone number for the client, so despite the late hour, David decided to give her a call to make sure Lizzie had made it to her house that afternoon. The line rang out; maybe she was in bed by now. Taking in a deep breath to calm him, David walked to the mirror. His tired eyes showed signs of stress and worry. The speckles of grey in his close-cropped hair would turn white if Lizzie didn't come home soon.

CHAPTER EIGHT

Lizzie Holland lay like a sack of potatoes in the corner of the sofa. Roy feared that he had not given her enough of the drug. Minutes had felt like hours as he had nervously waited for the Rohypnol to take effect. It was once Lizzie had tried to stand up that she had been overcome by lightheadedness and had fallen backwards onto the cushions. She had mumbled something and then swiftly fallen unconscious. Roy knew that he had to act fast. It would not be long before someone noticed that Lizzie had not arrived home. A rush of fear and excitement surged through his veins. Taking the corners of the large polyester throw that draped over the sofa, Roy wrapped Lizzie inside it. Dragging her body down into the dimly lit cellar, he carefully unwrapped Lizzie from the throw and took a moment to look at his victim. Like Snow White Lizzie was quite beautiful in sleep, and Roy could not resist leaning down to run his bitten fingernail over her cheek. Her skin was soft and plump, with a little flush of pink here and there. He had better get on with things; Prince Charming would be here soon enough.

Roy had been carefully planning this day for weeks. How he would trick Lizzie into the house and what the best sedative would be. Setting up the fake Facebook profile had been genius. He could not believe how easy it had been and how quick people were to accept a friend request from a stranger. Glancing around the dusty cellar, Roy checked that all his tools were close to hand. A trip to the hardware store had been enough to buy what he needed: cable ties, clear plastic bags, and some rope twine. The red headed shop assistant had been very helpful. The cold, grey stone walls of the cellar were thick enough to block out any noise although there were not any neighbours for miles.

Walking back over to where Lizzie's unconscious body lay, Roy rolled her onto her front and removed her white trainers and socks. Immaculate toenails were painted in a deep red to match her fingernails. With the largest of the cable ties, he fastened her ankles together tightly. Next, pulling her arms behind her, he used another cable tie, securing together her small wrists. Roy propped up Lizzie's lolling head onto a piece of foam with a hole in the middle that he had made earlier. He did not want her to suffocate. Not yet.

CHAPTER NINE

Lizzie woke up feeling sickly with the worst headache ever. There was a musty smell and something strange under her face. On opening her eyes and seeing nothing, she could feel that she was lying face down on the floor. Disorientated and fuzzy, Lizzie tried to move, causing searing pain to shoot through her already aching body. Her wrists and ankles were stinging, and panic surged in her heart as the reality dawned on her. She was tied up and could not move. Lizzie's breath quickened, and the rising dread rose like a wave as the familiar panic attack took over her body and mind. Breaking into a cold sweat, her body began to tremble. Frantically wriggling and trying to ignore the agony of the plastic ties cutting into her skin, she managed to roll herself onto her back. The room was in darkness, and the floor was cold even though she seemed to be lying on a thin blanket of some sort.

'Focus. Count to ten. Breathe. In and out, in and out'. Lizzie tried to calm herself. Her memory was blank, and she just couldn't remember how she had gotten there.

Panic began to rise once more, but Lizzie knew that if she was going to escape, then she must remain calm. Lizzie was going to get out of there. That was the one truth that she did know. 'If some madman thinks I am going to die here in this black hovel, leaving my beloved David alone, then he is sadly mistaken'. She told herself with conviction.

Lizzie has fully clothed apart from her bare feet. Instinctively she felt that she had not been sexually assaulted, but who knew what this crazy person or people had in store for her? They could come back at any moment; Lizzie had to do something and fast. Her eyes adjusted to the darkness, and she could just about make out a few unfamiliar shapes. The room she was in was cold, and as she shuffled her stiff body along the floor, she hit what felt like the bottom of a flight of stone steps.

'Where in hell am I?' she asked the darkness.

'You are in my cellar'. The voice that came out of nowhere made Lizzie scream, and her body convulse. Roy Peters was sitting in the far corner of the cellar wearing night-vision goggles. He had been patiently waiting for Lizzie to wake up. Watching her squirm and panic in her incapacitated state had given him great enjoyment. He was surprised that she had managed to wriggle to the bottom of the stairs all tied up as she was. Lizzie was a fighter. This was going to be fun.

Footsteps in the dark walked towards Lizzie. With sweaty hands around her arms, she was dragged away from the stairs. Heavy breathing and stale whiskey on his breath, her captor pushed Lizzie face down onto her front once more. Lizzie began to scream and struggle, tears of fear, anger, and frustration pouring down her face.

'Let me go! Please don't do this', Lizzie begged. 'I have a family; I have a life'.

The room lit up, and Lizzie screwed her eyes tight shut against the shock of the sudden brightness. Slowly she opened them again and tentatively lifted her head off the floor.

Before Lizzie could focus on her surroundings, all the air was suddenly stolen from her lungs as a plastic bag was put over her head and pulled tight across her face. Terror like she had never known gripped her entire being as Lizzie fought for air. Sucking in nothing but plastic through her nose and mouth, her eyes began to bulge, her lungs were on fire, and her body jerked. This was it, the end of her. Nothing had prepared Lizzie for the nightmare of what was happening. No matter how many horror movies she had watched and screamed at the victim to fight harder, when it was happening to you, it was all futile. Lizzie was alone in a cellar with a psychopath, and no one was there to save her.

As Lizzie began to descend into blackness, and her last breath was about to leave her body, the plastic bag was quickly ripped from her head. Lizzie deeply gulped in the beautiful air as it re-inflated her desperate lungs and she began to cough violently.

Repeatedly, Roy tortured Lizzie until she was utterly exhausted and on the brink of death. When Lizzie was just about to give up, the cellar suddenly returned to darkness and footsteps up the stairs meant she was alone.

A while later, Lizzie had recovered enough to be aware of warm dampness down below. She had wet herself, and the smell of urine strangely made her realise that she was thirsty.

CHAPTER TEN

Driving down the bumpy track towards Rowan Cottage, David Holland scanned the darkness for any sign of Lizzie or her car. This area was a lonely place with no other houses for miles. Just pitch blackness in every direction. The glare of the car headlights on full beam fell upon a red shape up ahead. As David got closer, he could see that it was a red car. Lizzie's car, parked in front of a slightly dilapidated cottage. Bringing his vehicle to a halt, David ran over to the red Fiat. Peering inside, he realised he had left his head torch in the glovebox. Once he had retrieved it, he could see that the car was empty, and the doors were locked.

'Why would the car still be here?' David whispered. Surely, she wouldn't have tried to walk home. Something was very wrong; he could feel it in his gut. Lizzie was still here somewhere.

Music broke the silence and made David jump. 'The self-preservation society' rang out from the mobile phone in his pocket. It was Amber, Lizzie's sister.

'Have you found her. Is she home?' the anxious voice asked. 'We are all out of our mind with worry here. Mum and Dad want to phone the police, but I've persuaded them to wait until we heard from you'.

David explained where he was and told Amber to stay calm. He would speak to the people who live in the cottage and ring Amber back with any news.

Rowan Cottage was in complete darkness, but as it was one-thirty in the morning, he was not surprised. Making his way to the window, David tried to peer inside, but the grubby net curtains obscured his already limited view. Knocking on the door seemed wrong and intrusive at this hour, but his missing wife's car was parked outside of that house, and David wanted answers.

After knocking and waiting, knocking, and listening, David was growing impatient. He walked through the overgrown garden, thankful that he was still wearing his thick polyester work trousers and steel toe capped boots. Around the back of the cottage was another dense patch of land. His head torch shone on a set of stairs that seemed to lead down to a lower part of the cottage.

Despite the torch, David found it difficult to navigate his way through the triffid-like nettles and prickles. What felt like broken bits of brick or stone was buried amongst the long grass and suddenly David tripped over. Landing heavily onto the jungle-like ground, his head torch hit a piece of sharp brick, and the light went out. 'Shit', cursed David as he struggled to pick himself up, his hands and face stinging from nettle stings and scratches.

It took some minutes for his eyes to adjust to the dark, but eventually, he could see the steps once more. Taking more care this time, he walked over to them and descended until he reached a steel door. There was no window, and the door had been locked from the inside. David banged furiously on the door and then placed his ear against the cold hard steel. Nothing. He could not hear anything but the sound of his own rapid breathing.

CHAPTER ELEVEN

Roy steadied himself against the kitchen counter, the whiskey glass in his hand shook as adrenaline coursed through his body. Just knowing that Lizzie was still down in the cellar, frightened and in his total control was thrilling. When he had slipped the bag over her head, it had been such a shock to Lizzie. Oh, how she had gasped and panicked, writhed like a fox in a trap. Those beautiful eyes, begging for life, and only he could give it or take it away. Like God, he would decide the moment of her death.

Lizzie had lost control of her bladder during the ordeal; the fear he had instilled in her excited him further. He would clean her up, give her a drink of water, and then leave her to calm down a bit. Then he would use the rope.

Rummaging through his mum's old clothes, Roy found a blue flowery skirt with an elasticated waistband. It would do. If Lizzie wet herself again, at least most of it would just end up on the floor. He could just strip her naked, but it was cold down there, and he didn't want her getting hypothermia and losing consciousness on him. Where would be the fun in that? He had no real desire to have sex with Lizzie either; it was the thrill of having control and inflicting suffering that aroused him.

With the skirt in one hand and a plastic cup of water in the other, Roy made his way back down the cellar stairs. Lizzie was still face down on the ground, shaking and sobbing. On hearing Roy's approach, she began to groan and roll about on the floor. Roy pulled her up into a sitting position against the cobwebbed wall.

Her swollen and red eyes glared at him. Taking a knife, he cut the ties that bound Lizzie's ankles together and then began to unzip her jeans. She shouted and pleaded for him to stop. He peeled her soiled underwear and jeans down her chubby thighs.

'Don't worry, Lizzie; I'm not going to rape you. That isn't why you're here'.

After slipping the skirt up onto her waist, he fastened new plastic ties around her ankles. Holding the cup of water to her lips, Roy could see Lizzie was afraid to drink. Her thirst soon overtook suspicion, and she greedily gulped down the water.

'Who are you? Why are you doing this to me?' Lizzie must have been feeling brave, he thought.

'I'm Roy, don't you remember Lizzie? All will be revealed in good time'.

Leaving Lizzie in the sitting position, he walked back up the cellar stairs and turned off the light. Just as he was about to walk away, Roy heard a loud banging on the outer door of the cellar that led into the back garden. He was here. He had found them. Roy knew that he would; he had counted on it.

CHAPTER TWELVE

David had just about run out of patience. Fighting his way back to the front of the cottage, he redialled the number that he had for Leanne Parker. From inside the house, he heard the bell-like sound of a telephone. No one came to answer it. No shadows passed the window, and no lights were switched on. Not knowing what to do next, David returned to his car and dialled 999. After answering a range of frustrating and pointless questions, he was informed that a couple of police officers would be sent to his location. David was told to wait in the car, and under no circumstances was he to attempt entry into the cottage.

Waiting for the police to arrive was torture. Lizzie was in that house, and God only knew what was happening to her. Maybe she was hurt or dead. David's mind was spinning with worst-case scenarios. Checking the time on his phone, he saw that it was two-twenty-seven am.

'What is taking the police so long? I've had enough of this shit', he said aloud. Opening the boot of his car, he pulled out a four-inch serrated fishing knife and marched determinedly over to the cottage. In a state of desperation, David tried the handle on the front door; to his surprise the door was unlocked. Using every inch of his old army training, David crept stealthily through the door and felt his way into the cottage. Every fibre of his body was tense and his senses on high alert. Fumbling around the walls with one hand, he found a light switch and flicked it downwards. Nothing happened. The cottage remained in blackness. If only the damned head torch hadn't broken.

Another idea immediately burst into David's mind. He would turn his car to face the windows and shine the headlights into the cottage. Retracing his steps, David could see the open front door, but before he could reach it, something hard hit the back of his head. Reaching up to touch the pain, David felt a warm liquid trickle through his fingers. Turning around, he saw what he could only describe as a dark figure with weirdly shaped eyes.

'Hello, David', said the figure. 'I've been expecting you'.

Bewildered and woozy David opened his mouth to speak, but another blow to the head knocked him cold to the floor along with his knife.

Returning the iron poker to the fireside, Roy sat on the sofa feeling rather pleased with himself. Snow White was in the cellar, and Prince Charming lay bleeding at his feet. Who would have thought it? Soft little Roy who everyone thought was pathetic had outsmarted an ex-army man.

'Not so tough now, are you David?' Scoffed Roy smugly. He would switch the electric back on and let David see just what 'fuckwit' Roy was capable of.

Onto a wooden chair brought in from the kitchen, Roy heaved up David's limp body. David was heavy, and Roy had to catch his breath before tying him to the chair with rope twine. He looked in a bad way. The blood was dripping in a line down his forehead, but he was still breathing. Roy would wake him up soon and then the real fun could begin. As soon as Roy had realised that David Holland had arrived at the cottage, it was time to put his cruel plan into action.

Turning off the electric and donning his night-vision goggles, he had lain in wait for David to enter the room.

Now it was time to fetch precious little Lizzie up to play the game called 'who will survive the longest?'

Lizzie heard the door at the top of the stairs open and began screaming and begging as Roy and his retro brown cords plodded towards her. At that moment, the fragment of memory flashed into her brain: the client: the creepy cottage: Roy. 'Oh my God!' Lizzie cried.

'Oh Lizzie, Lizzie, we're going to have some fun tonight, just the three of us. I just need to take a few bits and pieces upstairs then I'll come back for you'.

Roy's feminine voice sounded almost friendly like he was talking to his mother or someone.

'The three of us'. That was what he had said. 'Oh Lord no, please no'. Lizzie whispered in sheer desperation.

'There's another one up there, another evil bastard waiting to torture me again'.

Gathering more ties, a nail gun, and some plastic bags, Roy made a point of waving them in front of Lizzie as he made his way back up the stairs.

CHAPTER THIRTEEN

A glare of brightness caused David to jerk awake, and for a split second, he didn't know where he was. Throbbing pain in his head and blood on his hands was all it took for him to remember. The light was back on, and David's arms had been tightly tied to the chair that he was uncomfortably sitting on. Instinctively, he began to wriggle his arms from the rope causing his wrists to bleed. He felt sick and light-headed, but David knew he had to get free before that psycho came back. Something terrible had happened to Lizzie. Wherever she was, David had to find her. His beautiful, kind Lizzie; what if she was already dead? What if he was too late? Tears began to blur his eyes. 'No!' He said to himself.

With raging anger, he ignored the pain and furiously pushed his wrists back and forward against the rope, nervously glancing around the room for his attacker returning. A blood-stained iron poker left by an old fireplace caught his eye, and then something silver and shiny sticking up from underneath the sofa. It was the fishing knife! He must have dropped it earlier, and that maniac hadn't noticed.

Managing to semi-stand up while still tied to the chair, David awkwardly lay down on his side close to the blade of the knife and rubbed the rope against the edge. After what felt like an eternity, the rope severed, and he quickly released his other wrist. Picking up the knife, David moved slowly out of the living room and down a long hallway where a heavy-looking door at the end stood slightly ajar. Next to the door, leaning carelessly against the wall David recognised a twelve-gauge shotgun. Inching his way towards it, David caught a glimpse of what was behind the door.

Stone steps led down into what must be the room he had found at the back of the cottage earlier. Lizzie sat against a wall traumatised but alive. Her hands and feet were tied, and she was wearing some old-fashioned flowery skirt. She looked small and terrified; her eyes were bloodshot and swollen. At that moment, David had never felt more in love with Lizzie or more afraid that he could still lose her.

The back of a man suddenly came into view next to Lizzie, and David recognized the smarmy voice of his attacker as Roy taunted her. As quietly as possible, David put the knife in his pocket and picked up the shotgun, relieved to see that it was loaded. Knowing that this was his only chance before the blood loss from his head caused him to pass out again, David kicked back the cellar door and got into position.

The man who looked into David's eyes with shock and disbelief was not what David had been expecting. Although the man had spoken softly, David assumed he was a solidly built son of a bitch, not a flabby, ageing mummy's boy, but David wasn't going to underestimate the crazy fucker. Firing the shotgun with precision, he watched as Roy flew back down the stairs, and his insides gruesomely decorated the cellar walls.

CHAPTER FOURTEEN

Detective Chief Inspector Cathy Wallis sat at her desk and ran nicotine-stained fingers over her tired eyes. It had been a long night, and she was more than ready for her bed, but this paperwork wouldn't write itself. Earlier on there had been a few drunk and disorderly brought into the police station, but other than that, it was relatively calm. She was just about to grab herself another coffee when Sergeant Steve McNairy tapped on her door.

'Have you got a sec Ma'am?' he asked in his now slightly faded Scottish accent.

'What is it, McNairy? It's nearly two am, and I've not even finished this yet'.

'Yes, sorry Ma'am. It's just we've received a call about a missing woman. Her husband got home from work tonight, and she wasn't there'.

'For Christ's sake McNairy, she's probably off with her fancy man. How long has she been missing?'

'Thirteen hours Ma'am, but before you jump in again, the husband has found her abandoned car...outside Rowan Cottage'.

Cathy was suddenly wide awake. Rowan Cottage was the home of Roy Peters, a sad but dangerous little man with a penchant for cruelty and online stalking. He had previously been brought in for questioning over abusive and threatening behaviour on social media but had been released with a caution. Roy remained on their watch list though, as Cathy always believed that he was capable of something more sinister. He already had a juvenile record for killing a school friend's dog. Roy had claimed that the 'friend' had set the dog on him after an argument and that he only strangled the dog in self-defence. An eyewitness told a different story, and Roy was given a ban from keeping animals for ten years.

'Let's go and check it out', said DCI Wallis. 'I've got a bad feeling about this. You can tell me all the details on the way, McNairy'. Two cars had been parked up outside the cottage where Roy Peters lived alone. A red Fiat Punto and a white Nissan Juke. After asking for a vehicle check, it was established by dispatch that both cars belonged to Elizabeth and David Holland.

Sergeant McNairy pulled up behind the Nissan and turned off the engine. Stepping out of the car, they could see that the cottage lights were on, and they could not hear any disturbance from inside.

'Maybe it's a false alarm, Ma'am, or the wife is having it off with Roy'. Steve McNairy was thinking aloud, and DCI Wallis shot him a look of disbelief.

'Have you ever seen Roy Peters?' she asked. 'Elizabeth Holland would have to be blind for a start, and that's before she smelled his breath'.

Sergeant McNairy gave a slight smile behind his substantial brown beard.

A loud and sudden gunshot pierced the early morning silence instantly changing the atmosphere. Cathy's voice was serious.

'That came from inside the cottage'. She immediately radioed for backup.

'This is DCI Cathy Wallis with Sergeant Steve McNairy in attendance at Rowan Cottage, Brierley Lane, in Newsham requesting immediate backup and ambulance. Shots fired; I repeat shots fired at Rowan Cottage. Backup required immediately'.

'Do we go to Ma'am?'

'No, we stay here and wait for backup McNairy. We are unarmed and have no idea what's going on in there'.

CHAPTER FIFTEEN

Staggering down towards her was the man with the gun. His head was severely bleeding, and he seemed to be shaking. Lizzie began to sob uncontrollably as her bruised and bloodied husband wrapped his arms around her and pulled the fishing knife from his pocket.

'I'm so sorry, Lizzie. I should have found you sooner'.

David's voice was raw with emotion as he cut the plastic ties from her wrists and feet. Immediately Lizzie lifted a painful hand to the cut on his head. Her voice was hoarse.

'You're hurt, David. What did Roy do to you?'

'I'm alright, Lizzie. We need to get out of here. Can you walk?' Lifting her gently up off the floor, David helped his fragile wife to her feet. Lizzie glanced at the lifeless body of her captor as he lay sprawled in a pool of blood.

'What are we going to do, David? You've killed him'.

As if in answer to her question, a police armed response team appeared at the top of the stairs. Lizzie was once again facing the barrel of a gun. Urgent voices shouted a warning for them to stay where they were and to raise their hands above their heads. David turned his face to look at Lizzie one last time, smiled a little, mouthed 'I love you', and then fell heavily to the ground.

Following the armed response team into the cottage, DCI Wallis knew that something terrible had occurred in this house. The smell of blood, urine, and rot was prominent. Fresh blood pooled on the aged living room carpet, and a wooden kitchen chair lay on its side. The frayed pieces of blue rope twine still attached to the arms told a sinister story. Following the blood droplets led horrifyingly to a scene of devastation in the cellar. The walls splashed with red blood and pink flesh like a disturbed Jackson Pollock painting. The bodies of two men lay on the floor. Lizzie Holland stood with her trembling hands on her head, staring at the wall. Skin as white as death with bare feet and sunken eyes in shadowy sockets.

'Get an ambulance crew down here now!' ordered DCI Wallis.

CHAPTER SIXTEEN

L izzie screamed at David, and he could tell that she didn't immediately recognise him. His whole body had begun to shake, and he felt weak and sick. On unsteady legs, he made his way down the cellar stairs and knelt in front of Lizzie. At once, she was overcome with shock and emotion, falling forward into his arms like a helpless child. Not wanting to ask what she had been through, David proceeded to cut through the bonds that fastened her wrists and ankles together. Anger flashed through him as he saw the deep fissures in her skin. Lizzie's concern was immediately for him as her tender hand reached for his injured head. Her long-tangled hair fell away, revealing a painful-looking red line and purple bruising around her neck. Guilt and fury rose in David's chest. He didn't care what happened to himself; his priority was to get Lizzie out of this hell hole. The police would be here soon, and they would find the body.

As he helped Lizzie to her feet, his vision became blurry. Distant voices seemed to be telling him to do something, and it reminded him of being in the army. The last thing David remembered was Lizzie's pretty eyes before everything went black.

CHAPTER SEVENTEEN

Amber phoned David's number for the third time. No answer, and Lizzie's mobile was still going straight to voicemail. Shouting up the stairs to her parents, Amber tried to reassure them.

'Mum I've just spoken to David. Everything is fine, don't worry', she lied. 'I'll be back to see you in the morning to explain'.

Margaret and George Evans were almost seventy years old, and Amber didn't want to risk making them ill with worry unless she had to. Driving the short distance to Lizzie and David's house, she pulled up on the empty driveway. Both cars were gone, but Amber knocked on the door anyway. This was crazy. It was almost one-thirty in the morning. What was going on?

Remembering her last conversation with David, Amber followed the directions to Rowan Cottage in a desperate attempt to get some answers. Flashing blue lights illuminated the dark country lane, and a police officer motioned for her to stop the car.

'Can I ask why you are driving this way, Miss?' asked the solemn-looking young officer.

Amber explained, and afterwards, she thought she detected a hint of pity in the eyes of the officer.

'You had better come with me, Miss Evans'.

Dread lay heavily in the pit of Amber's stomach as she was led past police cars, ambulances, and then two cars which she recognised. Two body bags were wheeled out of the cottage by the ambulance crew, and at that awful moment, Amber lost the contents of her stomach.

'Lizzie, oh God Lizzie. I'm so sorry, please no'. She cried in anguish. Looking up, she saw a third person being brought out of the open cottage door. This time they were alive. An official-looking woman with short blonde hair, wearing a grey suit, approached the young officer, and Amber could tell that they were talking about her. The woman in the suit walked over.

'Miss Evans, my name is Detective Chief Inspector Wallis, I understand you are the sister of Mrs Elizabeth Holland?'

'Lizzie, yes that's right. She's my sister; please can you tell me what's happening?'

The DCI walked Amber over to the ambulance.

'Lizzie is inside. She was held captive in that cottage, and although we don't have all the details yet, we believe your sister has been subjected to a violent assault. I'm sorry to have to inform you that your brother-in-law David has been fatally injured'.

CHAPTER EIGHTEEN

Lizzie knew the moment that David collapsed beside her that he was dead. She saw the light leave his eyes and instantly felt her heart stop. In a state of numbness, Lizzie was vaguely aware of a commotion. People were shouting, fussing, and lifting her onto something. It was all a blur. Life no longer had any meaning now that David was dead. Her loving husband and best friend was gone. He had saved her life and lost his own. Salty tears began to fall as she remembered David's handsome smile. His hearty laugh and his silly sense of humour. How his hands were always warm. How he would shower her in kisses and tell her that 'he loved her more'. Lizzie wished that she had died too. She didn't want to go on in a world without David. He had been her everything, and they had been really happy.

This entire nightmare was all her fault; why had she left her perfectly safe job in the pharmacy to follow a stupid dream? David would still be alive if only she had listened to everyone.

'Why? Why didn't I listen?' Lizzie asked herself in despair.

CHAPTER NINETEEN

T he clinical white of the hospital seemed impersonal and cold. DCI Cathy Wallis' functional black shoes silently walked down the corridor and entered the room. Lizzie Holland was sitting up in a crisply made bed, staring blankly out of the window. The abundance of flowers and cards did nothing to brighten the solemn atmosphere. A tray with some uneaten sandwiches sat on the side table next to a standard blue hospital chair.

Cathy sat down and gingerly touched Lizzie on the arm to get her attention. Lizzie had already given a statement, and it had been decided that Roy Peters' death was carried out in self-defence and that he had killed David Holland. DCI Wallis was here today to inform Lizzie of the motive that drove Roy to target her and David.

After seizing his computer and digging into his online history, the police discovered that Roy and David had been involved in a long-running and heated argument about fox hunting. David had been a passionate animal lover, and the debate had turned increasingly nasty. After an insult where David had called Roy a 'pathetic little fuckwit', the argument appeared to have abruptly ended. However, Roy had taken that insult to heart as it brought back painful childhood memories of when he had been continuously bullied. He used the power of social media to find out everything possible on David Holland. His life had been easy to piece together from all the snippets of information posted online.

After seeing the profile of David's darling little wife, Roy plotted his revenge. The fact that Lizzie had a mobile business seemed almost too good to be true. Using the dark web, he was able to buy Rohypnol, known as the 'date rape drug'.

Setting up the fake Facebook profile of seventeen-year-old Leanne Parker, he went on to make an appointment for Lizzie to come to his house. The plan had been to hold Lizzie captive and torture her until David figured out where she was. Once he had both Lizzie and David in his control, Roy had planned various methods of pain for each of them in turn, forcing the other to watch. He would Lord it over David, making sure he understood exactly who Roy was and why he was doing this. Eventually, after making David beg for forgiveness, Roy would shoot Lizzie in the head.

David would suffer terribly, watching helplessly as the love of his life had her brains blown out. Roy had intended to taunt David, telling him how this was all his fault, before finally killing him too. No one will ever know if, or how, Roy had planned to get away with it.

CHAPTER TWENTY

A mber Evans had her sister all to herself again. It had been what she wanted but not like this. Lizzie had been inconsolable for a very long time after what happened to her and David. She attempted suicide more than once and spent many months in therapy.

It was difficult to know what to do or say to help her little sister. This unimaginable, terrible thing had happened to her, and nothing could make it better.

Rowan Cottage had been boarded up and would become the infamous horror house of legend and ghost stories for future generations. Amber fought to have it demolished; she wanted to wipe out any trace of that madman who had caused her family so much pain, but she had lost the campaign. She couldn't imagine anyone would want to buy and renovate the place to live in, not after they learned of it's tragic history.

CHAPTER TWENTY-ONE

Eighteen months later.

Lizzie Holland stood in front of the mirror. Her body was leaner now; her face was hardened. Cold, dead eyes that once were pretty stared back at the young widow. No longer weak and vulnerable, Lizzie had used her anger and grief to toughen up. Defined and strong muscles gave her an athletic appearance, and her mind was focused and disciplined. The scars on her neck and wrists had faded, hidden now by the shirt and long sleeves of her work uniform.

As she walked confidently through the station door, Lizzie felt a sense of purpose and she ignored the whispers behind her back. Everyone knew what had happened to her in that Godforsaken cottage. That's why she was there. Lizzie wanted to stop all the other Roy Peters that might be out there, scuttling and stalking in the darkness. Hurting innocent people and taking their hearts away. Joining the police force at her age had been a brave decision for Lizzie. Her steely determination would see her advance up through the ranks, eventually making detective. Once she had the power, DI Lizzie Holland would stop at nothing to bring every single one of those fuckwits down.

Printed in Great Britain
by Amazon

59449771R00033